P9-BZQ-550

The Cold & Hot Winter

BY JOHANNA HURWITZ

The Adventures of Ali Baba Bernstein
Aldo Applesauce
Aldo Ice Cream
Baseball Fever
Busybody Nora
Class Clown
DeDe Takes Charge!
The Hot and Cold Summer
Hurricane Elaine
The Law of Gravity
Much Ado About Aldo
New Neighbors for Nora
Nora and Mrs. Mind-Your-Own-Business
Once I Was a Plum Tree
The Rabbi's Girls
Rip-Roaring Russell
Russell Rides Again
Russell Sprouts
Superduper Teddy
Teacher's Pet
Tough-Luck Karen
Yellow Blue Jay

Johanna Hurwitz
The Cold & Hot Winter

illustrated by Carolyn Ewing

PALOS WEST LIBRARY
12700 South 104th Avenue
Palos Park, Ill. 60464

Morrow Junior Books
New York

Text copyright © 1988 by Johanna Hurwitz
Illustrations copyright © 1988 by Carolyn Ewing

All rights reserved. No part of this book may be reproduced or utilized in any form or by any means, electronic or mechanical, including photocopying, recording or by any information storage and retrieval system, without permission in writing from the Publisher. Inquiries should be addressed to William Morrow and Company, Inc., 105 Madison Avenue, New York, NY 10016.

Printed in the United States of America.

1 2 3 4 5 6 7 8 9 10

Library of Congress Cataloging-in-Publication Data
Hurwitz, Johanna.   The cold & hot winter.
Summary: Fifth grader Derek and his best friend Rory are delighted
when their neighbor's niece Bolivia comes to town for another visit, until
a lot of missing objects make Derek begin to doubt Rory's honesty.
Sequel to "The Hot & Cold Summer."
[1. Honesty—Fiction. 2. Friendship—Fiction] I. Ewing, C.S., ill. II. Title.
PZ7.H9574Co 1988   [Fic]   88-5144
ISBN 0-688-07839-7.

For Ilsa,
my friend through many seasons,
many years

Contents

The Cold & Hot Winter

1
Boxing Day

This year was special!

When Derek Curry went to bed on Christmas night, he felt the same wonderful anticipation that he had felt the night before. It had been exciting to lie in bed on Christmas Eve. He had heard the mysterious crackle of wrapping paper and the footsteps of his parents in the next room and wondered about the surprises waiting for him the next day.

But until now, Christmas night had always been a letdown. Even if he had received every gift he had ever wished for, and a few others besides, on Christmas night he knew

1

that nothing exciting was going to happen in his life until his birthday on May 4.

Derek turned over in bed restlessly and thought about his best friend and almost-next-door neighbor, Rory Dunn. The two boys were in the same fifth-grade class at the Woodside Elementary School, and they did everything together. Chances were that Rory was in his bed at this very moment thinking the very same thoughts that he was.

Both boys had been counting the days until December 26. Ever since their neighbor, Mrs. Golding, had told them that her great-niece, Bolivia, was coming to visit for a week during the winter recess from school, it was all they talked about. Although Bolivia Raab was exactly their age, Derek and Rory would never have met her if she hadn't spent last summer visiting her relatives in Woodside, New Jersey. Bolivia lived in upstate New York and until her visit, the boys had never heard of her. Now, months after she returned home, they still talked about her all the time. Bolivia was unlike any girl they had ever known before.

Derek heard the crackle of paper from the other side of his room. It wasn't his parents wrapping another gift for him. The sound was actually coming from one of his gifts. Derek had received a hamster in a cage from his parents. He couldn't wait to show off Hamlet to Bolivia the next day. He began counting what other things he had to show her. There were the new hockey skates that both he and Rory had gotten. (Their mothers often went shopping together.) He hoped Bolivia remembered to bring her ice skates.

He also hoped he would get a chance to spend some time alone with Bolivia. There was something important that he wanted to discuss with her. It was something he didn't want Rory to know he was going to talk about.

Bolivia was scheduled to arrive at two o'clock, and Mr. and Mrs. Golding had invited Derek and Rory to go to the airport with them. Derek had been to the airport a few times before. But he had never been in an airplane. When he had asked Bolivia last summer how many times she had flown to far-off places, she had not been able to say. Imagine flying more times than you could remember. And imagine that after so much traveling, Bolivia insisted that Woodside, New Jersey, was one of the best places she had ever been.

"Do you think she will have changed?" Derek whispered to Rory as they were driving toward the airport. They hadn't seen her for four months, and Derek worried that she might be different. Suppose they didn't like her anymore? Suppose she didn't like them?

Rory shook his head. "It's irrelevant," he said, using one of the big words that his father was always teaching him. "Even if she changes, she'll still be more interesting than anyone else we know."

"And more fun," said Derek, remembering their past adventures.

There was a lot of traffic around Newark Airport. "Look how many people are traveling," Mrs. Golding marveled. "I bet they are all going to Florida."

"Why does everyone want to go there?" asked Derek.

"They want to escape from the cold," said Mr. Golding. "I could use a bit of hot sun myself right now."

How silly grown-ups were, Derek thought. It was a cold day but that didn't bother him. Winter was supposed to be cold. And if they were lucky, they would get a couple of good snowstorms before the season ended.

Inside the waiting area, Mrs. Golding checked the flight board. "The plane is on time," she announced.

Derek had never even considered that it might be delayed. He had waited long enough for this moment. He could not bear waiting one minute more.

"Here I am!" Bolivia shouted as she pushed her way past the other passengers disembarking from the plane. She looked exactly as he remembered. Her red hair was poking out of a red-and-white woolen hat and she had a long red-and-white scarf hanging around her neck.

Mrs. Golding grabbed her great-niece in her arms for a big hug. Then Mr. Golding had his turn. Derek and Rory stood by, grinning self-consciously. They were glad to see their friend but they certainly weren't going to express it the same way old people did.

Bolivia grinned at them. "Happy Boxing Day!" she announced.

"What's that?" asked Derek.

"In England, December 26th is a national holiday. In the old days people gave their servants money in little boxes on the day after Christmas. So it got to be called Boxing Day."

Derek had forgotten that Bolivia always knew odd pieces of information. She was a walking trivia game. At first it had been irritating, but after a while, he realized that she was also very interesting. He had picked up a lot of unusual information last summer.

"We've got boxes for you at home," said Rory. "But they don't contain money."

"I've got boxes for all of you, too," promised Bolivia. "It's fun to have Christmas presents two days in a row."

"Where's Lucette?" asked Derek as Bolivia claimed her luggage. Lucette was Bolivia's pet parrot. She had come to Woodside with her last summer.

"I couldn't bring her because of the cold weather. Don't forget parrots are tropical birds." Then seeing the disappointed expressions on the boys' faces, Bolivia added, "But she sends you greetings. I taught her to say 'Happy New Year.' "

When they got to Woodside, they went to the Goldings' house where Bolivia distributed the gifts that were in her suitcase. There were packages containing red-and-white hats and scarves for both Derek and Rory. "Red and white are the Cornell colors," Bolivia told them.

Derek remembered that Cornell was the name of the college where Bolivia's parents taught.

The boys' gift for Bolivia was a poster-size blowup of a snapshot Rory's mother had taken of the three of them last summer.

"You can hang it in your room at home," suggested Derek as Bolivia unrolled the picture.

"Isn't it humongous?" asked Rory.

"No. It's us!" said Bolivia, and they all laughed. Humongous was another of Rory's grown-up words.

There was a second, smaller box for Bolivia.

"Chocolate toothpaste!" She giggled.

"It's from my father," said Derek, blushing. It was a silly gift, but when your father was a dentist, what could you expect? Both he and Rory had gotten identical toothpaste tubes in their Christmas stockings.

Bolivia opened the cap and sniffed. "Yummy!" she said. Derek felt loads better.

"Now you have to come to my house," insisted Rory. "I want to show you what I got yesterday. Besides, Edna is waiting to see you, too."

Edna was Rory's little sister.

When they got to Rory's house his mother gave Bolivia a hug. "Welcome back to Woodside," she said.

Rory's father taught at the Woodside Middle School, so he was home to greet Bolivia, too. Rory showed off his new hockey skates and his Walkman. "I can skate and listen to music at the same time," he bragged.

"You never saw anyone on a hockey team doing that," said Derek. He was hoping that he and Rory would get good enough to be on the hockey team by the time they got to the Woodside Middle School. But if Rory was skating to music, how could they practice together?

Bolivia put her hand into the pocket of her jeans. "I forgot to show you my neatest gift of all," she said. She pulled out a bright red Swiss army knife. "I've wanted one of these for years," she said. "But my parents never thought I was old enough. Look," she showed them. "It has so many parts to it."

Derek and Rory leaned over to admire the different blades and the tiny scissors that were all part of the knife.

"I've always wanted one of those," said Rory, taking the knife from Bolivia and running his fingers up and down the shiny red plastic. "Gee, you're lucky."

"Yeah," Derek agreed. He thought about how you would be prepared for every possible emergency if you had a Swiss army knife in your pocket.

Bolivia let Derek hold the knife, too. It felt good in his hand. Maybe he could convince his parents to give him one for his birthday. But May was so far off.

"I want to see," said Edna.

All this time, Edna had been following them around. But she hadn't said a single word. She was feeling shy.

"Knives aren't for little girls," said Bolivia, hugging her little friend.

Derek returned the knife to Bolivia and she put it back into her pocket.

Suddenly, Bolivia noticed a pile of wrapping paper and some empty boxes from yesterday's gifts on the kitchen counter.

"Let's wrap up some more packages," she suggested.

"What sort of packages?" asked Rory.

"Well, this is Boxing Day, isn't it? Let's put things in boxes and wrap them up."

"Like what?" asked Derek.

"Everything," said Bolivia. "Like this." She held up a book. "And this." It was an ashtray.

This was just the sort of great game that Bolivia was so good at inventing. They all rushed around the house looking for objects to wrap. Derek grabbed a large can of tomatoes that he saw sitting on the counter in the kitchen. Rory took the clock from beside his parents' bed and one of Edna's old dolls. Bolivia sat on the floor and wrapped each object in its own box. When she ran out of boxes, Rory found more in the basement. When they ran out of gift-wrap paper, Rory took the colored comic sheets from the huge stack of newspapers.

Derek tore off pieces of tape and handed them to Bolivia. She was good at wrapping, and the packages looked very intriguing. If you didn't know what had gone inside, you would really think that they were a pile of new presents for someone.

"Now what?" asked Rory when all the boxes had been filled.

"Now we must hide the boxes," said Bolivia.

"Why?" asked Derek.

"My parents always hide my presents," said Bolivia. "It makes the fun last longer."

She divided the boxes into three piles. "We'll all hide some," she said.

"Then will we look for them?" asked Rory.

You never knew the rules of Bolivia's games because she made them up as she went along.

"But if we hide them, then we'll know where they are," said Derek. He didn't like cheating and it seemed to him that it would be easy to cheat in this new game.

"Then Edna will look for the boxes," said Bolivia.

"I like this game!" said Edna, jumping up and down with excitement. She had contributed a book and a pair of shoes for Bolivia to gift wrap.

Derek, Rory, and Bolivia took the packages and went around the house hiding them. Derek stuffed one under the sofa in the living room. He put another behind the Dunn's Christmas tree and still another on the bookshelf in Rory's room upstairs.

13

When all the boxes had been put in secret corners of the house, the three friends sat on the living-room floor together. But before Edna could start looking for all of the packages, Mrs. Dunn came into the living room.

"I can't understand it," she said. "I'm sure I left a can of tomatoes on the kitchen counter. I need it for supper. I'm making spaghetti sauce but I can't do it without tomatoes. Will you please go to the store for me and get another can?"

"I saw the can," said Bolivia. "We wrapped it up as one of the Boxing Day gifts."

"Then I'm not losing my mind," said Mrs. Dunn, looking relieved. "I'm afraid I'll have to take it back from you now," she said.

Bolivia grinned. "It will take a few minutes," she said. "We have to find the boxes."

"Where are they?" asked Mrs. Dunn.

"Everywhere," said Derek.

"It won't take long," Bolivia reassured Rory's mother. "We'll all look. And Edna is going to help us, too."

So all of the children began searching for

the boxes they had hidden. Derek remembered that he had put a box behind the Christmas tree and another on the shelf in Rory's room. Then before he could remember the other places where he had stashed wrapped boxes, he found one that someone else had hidden behind the chest in Rory's room.

It wasn't long before they were all sitting on the living-room floor opening boxes. It wasn't quite as much fun as Christmas, but there was a bit of suspense as each of them wondered who would find the missing can of tomatoes.

"This would be interesting with spaghetti," observed Mrs. Dunn as she opened a package and removed her husband's bedroom slippers.

Quite by chance, Edna opened the package that held her doll. "Irene," she cried, grabbing her old treasure. And she cradled the toy as if she hadn't seen it for years.

"I found it!" called Bolivia triumphantly, and she held up the missing can.

"Thank goodness," said Mrs. Dunn. She

left the children opening the other boxes as she returned to the kitchen. It wasn't long before she was back.

"I don't suppose any of you have seen the can opener?" she asked.

Derek looked at Rory. Rory looked at Bolivia. Bolivia looked at Mrs. Dunn. "It's in one of the boxes," she said, giggling.

"What about the spaghetti? Did you wrap that, too?" asked Mrs. Dunn.

"Nope."

"Thank goodness for small favors," sighed Mrs. Dunn.

The children continued opening boxes. Rory found a tube of toothpaste. It was a traditional mint flavor, not chocolate. Derek found the clock and Bolivia found the ashtray. They came to the last box. "This must be it," said Bolivia. She handed the wrapped box to Mrs. Dunn. "Why don't you open it?" she offered. "Happy Boxing Day."

Mrs. Dunn smiled as she took the box. "Happy Boxing Day to you, too," she said as she removed the wrapping paper. Inside the box was a small pewter vase, which usually

16

stood on top of the fireplace.

"I won't be able to open a can with this," she said.

"Where is the can opener?" asked Derek.

"It must still be hidden around the house somewhere," said Bolivia.

Bolivia, Rory, Derek, and Mr. and Mrs. Dunn spent the next fifteen minutes looking for the missing box. Mrs. Dunn actually found another box in the hamper. But when she opened it, she found one of Edna's plastic drinking mugs.

Eventually, the problem was temporarily solved by Bolivia going next door to borrow her aunt's can opener. And before long, they could all smell the spaghetti sauce cooking in the kitchen. Rory asked his mother if Bolivia and Derek could stay for supper. But Mrs. Dunn said it was only fair that the Goldings should have their niece to themselves for a little bit. Derek went back to his home, too.

It was only while he was eating supper with his own parents that he remembered that Bolivia had never gotten to see Hamlet. It didn't matter. She was going to be around for a whole week. She had only been here one afternoon and already things had livened up, he thought. Whoever had heard of Boxing Day in Woodside? He realized, however, it would not be easy to speak to Bolivia alone. Rory would not want to be excluded from a minute of their time with her.

Just as he fell asleep that night, Derek thought of something else. He remembered that he had hidden a box under the sofa in Rory's living room. He had a feeling that inside that box was the missing can opener.

2
The Abominable Snow Person

The first thing Derek heard when he woke the next morning was a rasping noise. He hadn't heard it since last winter but it took just a few seconds for him to recognize what it was. It was the sound of a metal shovel scraping along the sidewalk. Someone was shoveling outside and that could only mean one wonderful thing: it had snowed during the night.

Derek leaped out of bed and pulled the curtain aside. Sure enough, he could see his father brushing snow off the car and Mr. Golding clearing a path along his walk. A few flakes of snow were still falling. Super! Up until now, there had not been any snow that winter at all. And now there was both snow and Bolivia. It would be a great day.

While Derek was getting dressed, he heard the phone ring. To his surprise, his mother shouted up to him, "It's for you."

Derek rarely got phone calls. Since his best friend lived two houses away, they didn't need to use the telephone. But it wasn't Rory on the phone. It was Bolivia.

"Hi," said Derek when he recognized her voice.

"Have you seen my knife?" she asked him.

"You mean the Swiss army knife that you showed us yesterday? Sure, don't you remember, we were all looking at it."

"I mean after that," said Bolivia. "It's disappeared. I thought I put it back into my pocket, but when I was getting ready for bed last night it was gone."

"It must have slipped out of your pocket," said Derek.

"I already called Rory and told him to look around his house," Bolivia said. "And he called back and said it wasn't there."

There was a moment of silence while Derek digested this piece of information. He remembered how much Rory had admired the knife yesterday. And he remembered some other things about his friend, too.

"Why don't we meet at Rory's house and look some more?" Derek suggested. "Maybe the knife slid under a chair or someplace where Rory didn't think to look."

"Okay," Bolivia agreed. "It's my favorite present. I've just got to find it."

"I know," said Derek. "I'll meet you in ten minutes."

It took Derek only eight minutes to gulp down a glass of orange juice and eat the bowl of oatmeal that his mother had prepared. She always made hot cereal for him on winter mornings.

"I'm off," said Mrs. Curry as Derek swallowed the last of his cereal. "Dad's outside waiting. We'll see you this evening."

Derek hardly heard his mother. He was too busy thinking about Bolivia's knife. Besides, he knew the holiday routine inside out. With both his parents at work, Derek always spent his vacation time with Rory.

Bolivia was already at Rory's house when Derek arrived. He brushed the snow off his jacket and cleaned his boots on the mat before he went inside. He was sorry that they had to waste time indoors. This was the perfect morning for playing outside. But of course, he wanted Bolivia to locate her missing knife.

"We have to retrace all my steps from yesterday," Bolivia said when she saw Derek. He followed her into the kitchen.

"This is where I was standing when I saw the wrapping paper and the gift boxes." She walked a couple of steps. "Then I sat down here and wrapped one of the packages."

"Wait a minute," said Rory. "How about when you were looking for the hidden boxes?"

"Or when Edna was following you around?" Derek remembered. It was not so easy to recreate exactly what they had done yesterday, after all.

Derek removed the cushions from the living-room sofa. He found two pennies, but

Bolivia's knife wasn't there. He hadn't really thought it would be. Still, it was a possibility. He looked over at Rory, who was flat on his stomach sliding his hands under the large chair in the corner.

"Not here," Rory said.

Derek stared hard at his friend. Rory looked away and said, "I'll look upstairs."

"Good idea," said Derek. He wasn't going to say anything, but he had a terrible feeling. Lately Rory had done some things that weren't very honest. They weren't federal crimes, but still, you shouldn't write spelling words on your hands before you take a spelling test. And there was one time recently when Rory had been downright dishonest. If he cheated at school, maybe he had also taken Bolivia's knife. It was horrible to think that your best friend could be a thief.

Derek decided not to follow Rory upstairs. "Let's look around down here," he said to Bolivia. He would give Rory a chance to get the knife from wherever he had hidden it the day before. Rory could pretend to find it and Bolivia would never know what had happened. Derek was sure that's what Rory was going to do. Then it would be over.

Derek and Bolivia searched all over the kitchen and living-room areas. Edna followed them around. "We are looking for my knife," Bolivia explained. "Did you see it?"

"I'll show you," said Edna, pulling Bolivia by the hand. She took her big friend into the kitchen and pointed to the drawer where all the tableware was stored. Bolivia opened the drawer and saw the forks and spoons and knives inside.

"See, there are lots of knives," said Edna, proud to have been helpful.

Bolivia gave the little girl a hug. Then she looked at Derek and sighed. "Don't you have any ideas?" she asked.

Derek shrugged his shoulders. He just couldn't tell on Rory. And at any moment, Rory might come running down the stairs with the red Swiss army knife in his hand. But a minute later, when Rory came down the stairs, he had nothing.

"I can't find it," he said.

"Are you sure?" Derek asked. Why was

Rory doing this? All fall they had talked about Bolivia's visit and now she was here and he was spoiling it. How could he have stolen her knife?

"Sure I'm sure," Rory protested. "That's the second time I searched the house for it. It's probably over at the Goldings'. You could have lost it over there, you know."

"I know," Bolivia sighed. "But I just sat and watched TV last night, and here we were running around. So it seems much more likely that I lost it here."

"Well, you didn't," said Rory. "Come on, let's go outside already. We're wasting the whole day. Next thing you know it will be time to go to bed."

Derek wanted to go outside, too. If Rory wasn't ready to produce the knife, there was nothing he could do. When he got Rory alone, he would speak to him. He put on his jacket and waited while Rory dug out his boots from the hall closet.

"Me, too," said Edna. "I want to play outside."

"You'll get hurt if we have a snowball fight," said Rory.

"Why don't you make a snowman?" suggested Rory's mother as she watched the children get ready to go out into the snow. "Then Edna could help you."

"A snowman! A snowman!" Edna shouted, jumping up and down with excitement.

"Wait a minute," protested Bolivia, zipping up her jacket. "Why do people always make snowmen? Let's make a snow woman."

"A snow woman! A snow woman!" shouted Edna.

"Who wants to make a snow woman?" Rory groaned. "That's stupid."

"Can't we just make a thing out of snow?" asked Derek. All this talk was silly. He didn't care what they made as long as they went outdoors. At this rate, it would stop snowing and melt away before they even got outside.

"I know," Bolivia shouted triumphantly. "A snow person!"

"A snow person! A snow person!" Edna shouted, jumping up and down again.

It was agreed. So the four of them went outside to begin building. It had stopped snowing, but there were about two inches of snow on the ground. And it was a heavy, wet snow that was good for packing and rolling into large balls. "Let's build the snowman right here," said Rory as they stood in his front yard.

"Snow person!" Bolivia corrected him.

"Last year when we made a snowman, we made it there. Let's make it in my yard this time," Derek suggested.

"I think we should make this snow person in my aunt's yard," said Bolivia. "Then it's in the middle, not closer to either of you."

"But closest to you," Rory pointed out.

"Sure, but I'm the guest and you're supposed to be polite to your guests," grinned Bolivia. She raced over to the Goldings' yard and selected a spot.

"What difference does it make?" Derek asked.

"Okay," said Rory, giving in. But when Bolivia wasn't looking he pulled Derek aside. "I have an idea about this abominable snowman," he whispered.

"Snow person," Derek corrected him. "What's your idea?"

"I'll tell you later," Rory mumbled under his breath as Bolivia came toward them.

"Come on, you guys, get to work."

"Stop bossing us around," said Rory, but he was suddenly in a good mood. Derek wondered what his friend was scheming now. And then he remembered again about Bolivia's knife, hidden somewhere in Rory's house.

"What are you dreaming about?" asked Bolivia.

"Nothing," lied Derek, and he began to make a ball out of the snow.

Edna pretended to help. She ran around in circles and tried eating some of the snow. The older kids stopped working to watch her and laugh.

By the time they had made as big a snow figure as they could and clothed it with Bolivia's woolen hat and scarf, they were all beginning to feel the cold. Derek's woolen gloves were soaked from melted snow and his toes felt like lumps of ice inside his boots.

"Edna looks like a real snow person," said Bolivia, pointing to the snow-covered child.

"I'm a snow girl," said Edna, and no one could disagree with that.

They went inside and Rory's mother made hot chocolate for all of them.

"They are predicting more snow for later in the week," she told them.

"Yippee!" Edna shouted, spilling some of her hot chocolate on her shirt.

Derek had thought that they would spend the whole day together. But it turned out that Bolivia's aunt and uncle had made other plans for the afternoon. They were taking their niece to visit some other relatives.

"They promised that it's the only time I have to go anywhere with them," said Bolivia. "They said the rest of the vacation is completely mine. So tomorrow we can go skating or build a whole city of snow people or anything else we want."

Derek was disappointed. Bolivia still hadn't been over to his house to see Hamlet. Surprisingly, Rory looked quite pleased by the news that Bolivia would be away during the afternoon. As soon as Bolivia left, Rory revealed his scheme.

"Let's move the snow person from the Goldings' front yard to mine," he said. "Bolivia will think that it walked from one place to the other."

Derek grinned. He could imagine Bolivia's surprise if the snow person was in a new spot. But then it occurred to him that once again Rory was managing to get his own way. The snow person would be in *his* yard, after all.

And that reminded Derek that he had to talk to Rory about the missing knife. He couldn't say anything in the house because he didn't want Rory's parents to overhear. But as soon as the boys were outside again, Derek turned to Rory.

"You stole Bolivia's knife," he accused his friend.

"I did not!" Rory said, looking shocked at Derek's words.

"Come off it, Rory, I know you took it. The question is, when are you going to give it back to her? Are you going to make her suffer thinking she's lost it the whole time she's here?"

"I didn't take it," Rory insisted. "What kind

31

of a friend are you, accusing me like that?" Rory's face was very red. It was impossible to know if it was from anger or from the cold. "You're abominable to even think I'd do such a thing," he said. He was using another of his big words.

"And you're abominable to steal from a friend," Derek shot back. He could use Rory's words, too. "I know how you can act sometimes. And you know what I'm talking about. If you don't give the knife back to Bolivia tomorrow, then I'm going to tell what I know about you."

"Listen, that's blackmail," screamed Rory. "But it won't work because I tell you I didn't touch Bolivia's knife. I mean I touched it when she showed it to us. But I didn't take it. I swear I didn't take it. Besides, I saw how much you liked that knife yesterday. How do I know you didn't take it and now you're trying to put the blame on me? We should have gone and searched *your* house this morning," Rory shouted at Derek.

Rory turned his back on Derek and began digging around the base of the snow person.

Derek didn't feel like playing in the snow with him anymore, but he didn't know what else to do. He needed more time to think about the situation. He watched as Rory struggled, trying to lift the snow figure from its resting place in the Goldings' front yard and carry it to his own.

Reluctantly, Derek moved to give Rory a hand. As he staggered under the heavy load, a great idea suddenly came to him. Tonight, when no one was around, he would come back and secretly move the icy figure one more time. He would put it in his own yard. That way, both Bolivia and Rory would be surprised tomorrow morning. And with that thought in mind, he cheerfully helped Rory anchor the snow person in its new site.

"Listen," he said to Rory. "I'm sorry I accused you of taking the knife."

"Yeah. It was a pretty mean thing to say," Rory replied.

"I'm sorry," Derek repeated again. "If you didn't take it, I shouldn't have said it." But if you did take it, you are a rat, he thought silently to himself. He would have to search

33

secretly for the knife on his own. The awful thing was that he didn't want to prove that his best friend was a liar and a thief. But he had to think about Bolivia. She was his friend, too.

"Right." Rory readjusted the hat and scarf on the snow person. "Come on," he said. "Let's go inside."

Derek followed.

3
A Few Small Thefts

Despite his apology, Derek was certain of two things: that Rory had stolen the knife and that it was hidden somewhere inside the house. And he was determined to find it.

Although he had never bothered to add up the time, Derek was sure that over the years he had spent as many hours in Rory's home as he had in his own. As a result, he knew his way around the Dunn house. Now he wondered what would be the best way to go about searching Rory's house for the Swiss army knife.

Among Rory's Christmas gifts was a new board game from his grandparents. The two boys settled down on the living-room floor to play. But the instructions were so complicated that before long Rory called his father in for a consultation. Mr. Dunn sat down on the floor and began studying the rules together with his son. This was his chance, Derek thought.

"I'll be right back," he said as he went toward the stairs. They would think he was in the bathroom, but he had other plans. Quietly, so as not to wake Edna, who was napping in her room across the hall, Derek tiptoed into Rory's bedroom. Because the sky outside was overcast, the light was dim inside the room. Derek knew he couldn't turn Rory's lamp on. But he knew his way around the room without lights. The problem was, where would his friend have hidden the knife?

Derek stood in the middle of the room and tried to think what he would do if he had stolen something.

Under his underwear! That was a good possibility. Quietly, Derek slid open the top drawer of Rory's chest. Socks, undershirts, and shorts were all squeezed into the drawer in a mess. Derek moved his hand underneath the underclothes. He felt something hard and smooth and pulled it out, convinced he had found the missing knife. But when he saw what was in his hand, he was surprised at his mistake. He was holding the small plastic flashlight that Rory had gotten last year at the circus. Derek had one just like it at home. He clicked it on and was pleased to see that the flashlight still worked. He had never replaced the original batteries in his light. He didn't even remember where he had put it.

"Derek, what's taking you so long?" Rory's voice called up the stairs.

Derek tiptoed out of the bedroom and slipped into the bathroom. As he leaned over to flush the toilet (he knew from the movies that he had to cover his actions by making the appropriate noises), he realized that he was still holding Rory's flashlight. There was no time to put it away now. He slipped the flashlight into a pocket in his jeans. He would put it away when he went searching in the bedroom again. And the next time, the flashlight would come in handy to help him look.

"My father says he thinks this game will work better if there are three or four players," Rory explained when Derek entered the living room again. "Let's wait and play it tomorrow when Bolivia is here."

"Okay," said Derek. He hadn't especially wanted to play, anyhow. "How about going over to my house?" he suggested. "We can play with my hamster."

Rory agreed and the two boys put on their jackets and boots again.

"Did either of you see a pile of loose change that I left on the kitchen counter?" asked Mrs. Dunn as they were zipping up their jackets.

"No," said Derek, shaking his head.

"Me neither," said Rory.

Derek wondered if Rory had pocketed his mother's change. If his friend would steal Bolivia's Swiss army knife, why wouldn't he also take money?

"It was about three dollars' worth of quarters and dimes," sighed Mrs. Dunn. "I don't understand how it could disappear."

The door banged behind them as the two boys walked toward Derek's house. Rory stopped for a moment to admire the snow person.

"Boy, will Bolivia be surprised when she sees this has walked over to my house." He laughed.

Derek laughed, too. He was thinking how surprised Rory would be when he woke up tomorrow and the snow person had taken *another* walk.

Up in Derek's room Hamlet was sound asleep. But the little hamster woke up when Rory opened the cage door.

"He's really cute," Rory said. "Too bad he isn't a dog, though. Then you could teach him tricks and he could play with us outside."

"I bet I can train him to do some things," said Derek. "Look at this," he said. He put Hamlet on the wheel inside his cage. The hamster immediately began to climb around and around the wheel, making it move.

"See," said Derek.

"That's not exactly a trick. He probably was

PALOS WEST LIBRARY
12700 South 104th Avenue
Palos Park, Ill. 60464

born knowing how to do that."

Rory put his hand inside the cage and removed Hamlet. "He sure is soft, isn't he?" he said, gently stroking the light brown hair on the hamster's back.

After a while, the boys returned Hamlet to his cage. They went down to the basement and played Ping-Pong. Derek won two games out of three. The boys were just beginning a fourth game when they heard the sound of Derek's parents at the door.

"Hi, fellows," Mrs. Curry greeted them. "I've got a pot of beef stew that just needs to be heated up. Do you want to stay for dinner, Rory?"

Derek watched as his friend mentally balanced the advantages of beef stew over the meat loaf that his mother was preparing at home. Beef stew won and Rory stayed for supper. It was a good move because there was also apple pie for dessert. But for once, Derek was eager for his friend to leave. He wanted his friend to be tucked away in his own home so he could arrange to secretly move the snow person.

At last, around eight o'clock, after they had fed and petted the hamster a second time, Rory returned home. No sooner had the door closed than Derek went to his father.

"Dad, will you help me play a trick on Rory?" Derek explained how Rory and he had moved the snow person from the Goldings' yard during the afternoon. "Now, I want to move it again," Derek said. "But I will need help."

Dr. Curry laughed. "Sounds like a great idea," he said, putting on his jacket and boots.

Outside, it looked beautiful. The snow still clung to the branches of the trees and the light from the streetlamps cast a mysterious glow on everything. Dr. Curry took the shovel he had left in front of the house that morning and followed Derek to his friend's yard. Derek had worried that someone would see them, but there was no one about. An occasional car passed on the street, but otherwise, all was quiet.

As they passed the Goldings' house, Derek saw that the lights were on. Bolivia had returned from visiting her relatives. He wondered if she had entered the house through the garage or through the front door. If it had been through the garage, she might not have noticed that the snow person had vanished from the yard.

The blinds were closed in the Dunns' living room. A blue glow showed that the television set was on. Derek imagined Rory and his parents sitting together watching a program. The snow person was standing guard near the front door. The woolen hat was at an angle on its head and the long striped scarf hung down toward the ground.

Dr. Curry dug out around the base of the figure. "I wonder if you could get arrested for this?" he said. "Stealing a snowman."

"It's not a man," Derek said. "It's a snow person." He paused for a moment. "Could we get arrested?" he asked.

"I was only joking," his father said. "Someone has to press charges first and I don't think the Dunns would accuse us of theft."

With his father's help it didn't take long to

move the snow person from the Dunn yard to the Curry yard. Derek adjusted the scarf and the wool cap on the head of the snow person for the third time that day. He grinned at his father. And his father smiled back at him.

"Not bad," said Dr. Curry. "I never was an accomplice to a crime before, but I think we did a pretty good job."

"I wonder what Rory and Bolivia will think when they see this tomorrow," said Derek as he brushed snow off his jacket.

"They are predicting more snow before the week is out," said his father. "There may be enough snow for you to make snowmen in every yard on this street."

"Not men, Dad. This is a snow person," Derek explained again as they went inside.

"It's almost time for bed," Mrs. Curry called to Derek.

"Mom, don't forget this is my vacation," he reminded her. But all the playing out in the snow had made him tired. "I'll read in bed," he suggested as a compromise.

As he was undressing, Derek felt an unexpected lump in the pocket of his jeans. It was Rory's flashlight. He had forgotten all about it. He took the flashlight and hid it under his T-shirts in his chest of drawers. When he got a chance he would return it to Rory's drawer. But he doubted that his friend would miss it. He probably didn't even remember where he had put it.

Derek took a bath and put on his new, bright red flannel pajamas (a present from his grandparents). Then he took his copy of *The Lion, the Witch and the Wardrobe* (a present from Rory's parents) and got into bed. He read two chapters before his eyelids started to close.

As he began to doze off, he thought about how lovely and quiet it had been outdoors. It was silent in his bedroom, too. Hamlet must have been sound asleep already. There wasn't a noise at all from his cage.

Derek wondered what Rory would say tomorrow morning when he discovered that *his* snow person had taken a walk. He grinned with anticipation as he fell asleep.

4
Where Is
Hamlet?

The telephone rang while Derek was eating breakfast. It was Rory.

"How come you're calling?" asked Derek. "Why don't you just come on over?"

"I looked out my window and that abominable snowman has disappeared!" he said. "What do you think happened?"

"Big Foot walks again," said Derek.

"I don't understand it," said Rory.

"Come on over here," suggested Derek. "We'll investigate the mystery together." He smiled as he spoke. Wouldn't Rory be surprised to find the snow person standing in front of *Derek's* house!

"Okay. See you in a couple of minutes," said Rory.

The telephone rang again. This time it was Bolivia.

"What's taking you so long?" she asked. "You guys sure are slow getting started in the morning."

From where he stood speaking into the phone, Derek could see the kitchen clock. It was only eight-fifteen. Bolivia certainly didn't waste a minute.

"What's your hurry?" he asked. "We haven't even decided what we're going to do today." He paused for a moment. "Rory's coming over here. And you should come, too. You haven't seen my hamster yet." Or the new location of our snow person, he thought to himself.

"All right," said Bolivia. "But first come here and have a hot corn muffin. My aunt just baked them."

"I've practically finished my breakfast already," said Derek, looking at his bowl of cooling cereal. If the phone hadn't kept ring-ing he would have been done by now. "You should have called earlier, slowpoke."

"It doesn't matter," said Bolivia. "When you smell them, you'll find room for one of these muffins. And there's homemade strawberry jam, too. I just called Rory. He's on his way over."

Derek liked corn muffins, but he didn't think he would enjoy one after his bowl of cereal. On the other hand, Bolivia was only here for a few days and if it made her aunt happy to feed them muffins first thing in the morning, he'd stuff one down.

"See you tonight," he shouted to his parents, who were upstairs.

"Derek," his father called to him as he started out the door.

"Yes?"

"Don't be disappointed if your plan didn't work out quite the way you expected."

"What do you mean?" asked Derek. He didn't know what his father was talking about.

"You'll see when you get outside."

Derek quickly zipped up his jacket and opened the front door. He looked around. The snow person had disappeared. It was not in front of the house where he and his father had set it down the night before. The air was too cold for it to have melted. He didn't know what could have happened.

Slowly, he walked down the path from his house and across the Goldings' snow-covered lawn. There, standing right at the entrance to the Golding house, were Rory and the snow person. The latter was standing exactly where it had been when they had finished creating it the day before. How had it gotten back again?

"Well, I guess the mystery is half-solved," said Rory. "Now we know where the snowman is."

"Person," Derek corrected him. "But we don't know how it got here."

"Did you move it?" Rory asked his friend.

"No," said Derek. But of course, as he denied it, he realized that he was lying. He *had* moved it. He just hadn't moved it here.

"It must have been Bolivia," he said. "She must have moved it back."

The door to the Goldings' house opened. "What are you doing standing out here?"

49

asked Bolivia's aunt. "The muffins are getting cold. Come on inside."

Sitting at the kitchen table were Bolivia and her uncle. There was a platter of pale yellow muffins in the center of the table and they were each eating one. Bolivia smiled at her friends. Derek remembered an expression that he had heard used when a person looked very innocent. "Butter wouldn't melt in her mouth." That's the way Bolivia looked. The butter might be melting on her warm corn muffin, but it wouldn't melt in her mouth.

"You did it, didn't you?" Rory accused her. "You moved the snowman last night."

"Snow person," said Bolivia. "What are you talking about?"

"How did the snow person get in front of your house?" asked Derek.

"Don't be silly," said Bolivia, swallowing a mouthful of muffin. "That's where we built it. Of course it's in front of this house."

"Sure it is," said Mr. Golding. "What did you expect?"

At that moment Derek knew that Mr. Golding had been Bolivia's accomplice, just the way his father had been his. They must have gone out after he had gone inside last night. It had been foolish of Rory and him to think they could pull something over on Bolivia. She always came out on top!

"The weatherman says it's going to snow again," said Mrs. Golding.

Derek nodded as he bit into a muffin. "My dad said so, too."

"Let's go ice-skating today," suggested Rory. "We won't be able to skate later if there's snow on the ice."

"First you have to come over to my house," Derek protested. "Bolivia still hasn't seen Hamlet."

"Yes, I did," said Bolivia. "I saw a production of it up in Ithaca. It's a play by Shakespeare."

"This Hamlet is a hamster," said Derek. "Rory's father told us about the play. I was going to call my hamster Harry, but he said that Hamlet would be a much more distinguished name."

"Does he act distinguished?" asked Bolivia.

"He's smart," said Derek. "Wait till you see how he acts when I feed him."

"Big deal. When you feed him, he eats," said Rory.

"He stuffs his food into pouches in his cheeks," said Derek. "Then he can eat it slowly when he wants it." He was wishing he could stuff the rest of his corn muffin into a pouch so he wouldn't hurt Mrs. Golding's feelings. He was too full to finish it.

"Okay, let's go," said Bolivia. "First we'll visit Hamlet and then we'll go skating."

There was no one home at Derek's house when the trio arrived. Dr. Curry and his wife had left for work.

"Wait a minute," said Derek as Bolivia and Rory started up the stairs to his bedroom. "Let me get some food for Hamlet."

Derek went to the refrigerator and removed a leaf of lettuce and a piece of a carrot. "How would you like this for breakfast?" he asked his friends.

"Not me," said Rory.

"They eat salad for breakfast in Israel," Bolivia informed her friends. "The summer my parents were working on a dig there, we had tomatoes and cucumbers and radishes for breakfast every morning."

The boys made faces at the Israeli menu. Bolivia had certainly been to a lot of places and done a lot of weird things.

They went upstairs and Derek showed Bolivia the little cage that he had gotten with his hamster. It was made of wood and wire, with a pile of shredded newspapers on the cage floor.

"Come on, lazybones," said Derek, opening the side of the cage and moving his hand through the papers.

He found an uneaten piece of carrot, but there was no trace of Hamlet.

"I don't understand it. He's not here!" said Derek.

"Are you sure?" asked Bolivia.

"Yes. Look for yourself. There's nothing in the cage but newspaper. He's vanished," he said.

"He's bound to turn up somewhere. Just like our snowman," Rory reassured him.

"Snow person," said Bolivia.

Derek sat on the floor, stunned. "I don't know where he could be." What with Rory staying for supper last night and then the business of moving the snow person and reading in bed, the last time Derek had seen the hamster had been when the two boys had played with him before Rory had gone home.

"He probably got out of the cage and is under your bed or somewhere like that," said Rory. "Come on, we can all search for him."

Rory got down on his hands and knees and looked under Derek's bed. "It's dark under here," he said. "Give me a flashlight."

"I don't have one," said Derek. He was feeling miserable. A hamster wasn't quite as good a pet as a dog, but in the few days that Hamlet had been here he had grown very fond of the small furry creature.

"What happened to that little one we got at the circus?" asked Rory.

"It doesn't work anymore," said Derek.

"I can get mine," offered Rory. "I'll run home and get it. Hamlet is so tiny that he could be hiding in some dark corner. The only way we'll be able to see him is if we have enough light."

"That's a good idea," Bolivia agreed.

Derek froze. He suddenly remembered that he had taken Rory's flashlight from his drawer yesterday. "No, don't go. Stay here and help me look," he said. "I think my father has a flashlight I can get."

He went out of the room to look for the light his father kept in case of emergency. Flashlight in hand, he returned to find both Rory and Bolivia crawling around on the floor of his room.

"Shine the light in here," instructed Bolivia, pointing to the floor of his closet. "This is the perfect hiding place for a hamster."

They found the left sneaker of an old pair, which had been missing for several months, seventeen cents that must have fallen out of a pocket, and a pile of old games that Derek had outgrown and not played with in three years. But they did not find Hamlet.

"There's no reason why he had to stay in this room," said Rory. "Just because he be-

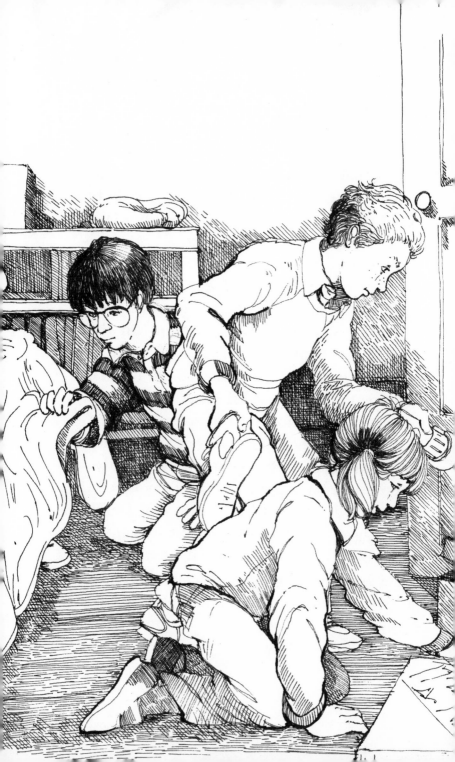

longs to you, he doesn't have to stay in here. He could be anywhere in the house."

"I'm glad you don't have a cat," said Bolivia.

Derek hadn't thought of Hamlet being in any real danger. Now he began to really worry. Suppose they didn't find him and he starved to death or died of thirst?

"How do you think he got out, anyway?" called Bolivia from the hallway, where she was crawling around on her hands and knees.

"I don't know," Derek said. "I closed the cage when we finished playing with him yesterday. You saw me, didn't you?" he asked Rory.

"Well, actually I didn't," said Rory. "I just assumed you did. But maybe you only shut it and it wasn't latched tight enough." He shrugged his shoulders.

After forty-five minutes of searching the Curry house, Bolivia came up with a suggestion. "Why don't you put the lettuce inside the cage and leave the door open. Maybe Hamlet will return on his own while we go skating."

"Maybe he won't," said Derek glumly. He wasn't in the mood for skating anymore.

"We've already looked everywhere," said Rory.

"We can't have looked everywhere because if we did we would have found him," Derek declared.

"If we go skating," said Bolivia, "it will clear our heads. We'll probably think of other places to look when we come back. This way we just keep retracing our steps and we aren't being successful at all."

"Suppose Hamlet is lost in another room and he can't find his way back," protested Derek. "He'll starve to death before we find him."

"Maybe he went off with his pouches stuffed with food," offered Rory. "Then he wouldn't starve at all."

"And maybe his pouches were empty," said Derek.

"I have a plan," said Bolivia. "Let's leave bits of food around the house. That way, wherever he is, he can find something to eat and it will also lead him back to his cage. Sort of like Hansel and Gretel," she added.

Derek smiled at Bolivia. He should have known she would come up with a solution. He started tearing the lettuce leaf into small pieces. If he left some in his parents' bedroom and some in the hallway and some in the bathroom . . .

"I'll get another leaf," said Bolivia. She went downstairs to the kitchen. Then she began distributing bits of lettuce around the ground floor.

Derek followed his friends downstairs. There was nothing else they could do now but wait. Rory and Bolivia put on their jackets and picked up their skates. Slowly, Derek did the same. He kept his eye on a piece of lettuce near the doorway. It would be wonderful if Hamlet suddenly appeared and began eating it.

But the pale green lettuce remained on the dark crimson carpet untouched.

"Cheer up," said Bolivia as they went out the door. "Hamlet will return. I'm positive of it."

5
The Hard, Cold Facts

B olivia had been right.

The cold air, the new ice skates, and the excitement of showing off on the ice all served as excellent distractions. Derek had skated all fall with rented skates. Now, wearing his own skates for the first time, he felt more confident on the ice than ever before. The new skates fit better and gave his feet more support. Derek whizzed past his friends on the ice. He felt as if he could skate forever. But after a few fast laps gliding in and out of clusters of kids, he rejoined his friends.

When they skated together, Derek knew they looked like some sort of team. Bolivia had retrieved her striped hat and scarf from the snow person, and all three of them were wearing their matching sets.

"I hope our snow person isn't cold today without its scarf and hat," said Bolivia.

"If it keeps walking up and down our street, then the exercise will keep it plenty warm," observed Derek. He was sorry that Bolivia didn't know he had moved the figure in the night. And he was sorry that Rory didn't know that he had moved the snow person last night either. It had been a wasted effort. Still, it had been fun to be out playing in the dark with his father. Maybe it wasn't a total waste of time, after all.

"You're not thinking about Hamlet, are you?" asked Bolivia as the three of them circled the rink.

It was the wrong thing to say. Immediately, Derek began to think about his lost hamster again.

"It's really weird how we both lost our favorite Christmas presents," Bolivia commented.

That was the wrong thing to say, too. It

reminded Derek how suspicious he was of Rory. He couldn't help it. Where else could the knife be if Rory hadn't taken it? And come to think of it, Rory had played with Hamlet last night. Could Rory have put the little animal inside his pocket and taken him home?

It just didn't make sense. It was one thing to hide a Swiss army knife in a drawer under your clothes or in your closet. How could Rory expect to hide a hamster and not expect to have it discovered?

Rory suddenly called out, "I'll race you guys to the refreshment stand." He took off and Derek and Bolivia followed quickly behind him. It wasn't a matter of who could skate the fastest. It was who could find a space within the crowd to skate through.

When they were sitting and sipping their hot chocolate, Derek began to think about Hamlet again. Could Rory possibly have done such a thing?

"What are you thinking?" Bolivia asked, poking Derek for attention.

Derek gave a jump and a little of the hot

liquid spilled from his Styrofoam cup. "What did you say?" he asked.

"Stop daydreaming," said Bolivia. "If it doesn't snow, what do you think about our skating tomorrow morning at eight o'clock? It will mean that you have to get up extra early, but then the rink won't be so crowded."

"Sure," Derek agreed. At least he didn't have to worry about Rory stealing his ice skates, since he had a brand-new pair of his own. Derek wished he could ask Rory outright: Did you take Hamlet? He didn't know why he was so afraid. Maybe it was because he didn't want to hear the answer. What would he do if his best friend said yes? What would he do if Rory said no, but the answer really turned out to be yes?

"There you go, daydreaming again," Bolivia complained good-naturedly. "Come on. Let's get back out on the ice."

Derek threw his empty cup into the garbage bin and walked back out to the ice. Maybe he would have a chance to ask Bolivia for advice. Bolivia always seemed to have an answer for everything.

As they skated off together, Derek noticed a couple of girls from school. "Look," he said to Rory. "There's Traci and Erin skating over there."

"I'll be right back," said Rory, skating over to the girls. Derek knew that Rory sort of liked Traci. He watched as Rory tried to spin around on his skates and impress the girls.

"How come you're so quiet these days?" demanded Bolivia. "Last summer you used to talk a lot."

Derek blushed. He wished he had the nerve to tell Bolivia what was troubling him. Then he had an idea. He would make his problem seem as if it belonged to someone else. Then it would be easier to talk about it.

"I was thinking about two fellows I know at school," he said as they skated off together. "They went to the supermarket to do some shopping for one of their mothers. When they got there, they were kind of fooling around. One guy got into the shopping wagon as if he were a baby, and the other fellow pushed him through the store."

"So?" asked Bolivia. "I've seen kids do that

lots of times. What's so special about that?"

"Well, that's just the beginning," said Derek. "As they went past the shelves with the salad dressings and stuff, the guy who was pushing the wagon lost control and he banged into a shelf. He knocked a bottle of cooking oil onto the floor. The bottle broke and the oil spilled all over."

"So?" asked Bolivia, puzzled.

"So what do you think they should have done about that?" asked Derek.

"I guess they should have gone to someone and told them about the accident. Otherwise, with that oil on the floor, other people might slip and fall and there could be a more serious accident."

"That's what I told Rory," said Derek, delighted to hear his own opinion seconded by someone else. "But he said that if we told, they would make us pay for the oil and we'd get in a lot of trouble."

"So what did you do instead?" asked Bolivia.

"Rory jumped out of the wagon and we quickly finished our shopping. Luckily, no one had been around when the bottle fell, so I don't think anyone knew that I did it. But I did feel pretty bad about the whole thing."

"It does sort of make you a hit-and-run driver, I suppose," said Bolivia. "But I don't think you have to go around feeling guilty about it for the rest of your life."

Derek nodded his head. "It's not just that," he said. "It's a lot of other little things. And some things not so little."

"You mean you have been living a life of crime since I last saw you—knocking bottles off shelves and doing other mean and nasty things?" Bolivia teased him.

"Yes," said Derek. "I mean, no. I mean, mostly I haven't done anything but . . ."

"But what?" asked Bolivia, looking confused.

Derek took a deep breath. How could he say it? But if he didn't talk about this with Bolivia, who would he talk to? "Look," he said. "I know he's my best friend, but I just have to tell someone. Lately Rory has done more and more things that are dishonest. Mostly he exaggerates or he tells little lies or

67

he doesn't admit things, like when we broke the bottle in the supermarket. But he did do one *really* dishonest thing, and ever since then I just can't trust him. I know it sounds awful to say this, but I think he stole your Swiss army knife. And the more I think about it, the more I think that he took Hamlet, too."

The words were out. He had finally said them. Derek turned to look at Bolivia to see how she was reacting to all this.

"I can't believe it," she said. "Why would he do a thing like that? It doesn't make sense."

"I know," admitted Derek. "But you lost your knife at his house and he was the last one to handle my hamster and now both are gone."

"That's just circumstantial evidence," said Bolivia. "You don't have any real proof."

"I know. It's just a feeling. But you haven't been around here all fall and listened to him. He lies to our teacher, he lies to his parents. Why shouldn't I think he would lie to me, too?"

"What's the big thing that you said he did?" asked Bolivia.

Derek looked around. He saw Rory was still busy skating with Traci and Erin. In fact, it looked like he was trying to teach the girls how to skate backwards, which wasn't easy because the rink was so crowded.

Derek took a deep breath and licked his lips. After keeping this secret for so long, it wasn't easy to say it aloud. "We had a special Balloon Day at school this fall. The Parents Association sold helium balloons to the students for a dollar apiece to raise money. If you bought a balloon, you were given a postcard on which to write your name and address and a message. The message asked whoever found the postcard to mail it back to you. The postcards were attached to the balloons and then we released all of them in the school yard at the same time. It was really a great sight to see four hundred balloons, all different colors, suddenly go flying off over the school building and into the sky. A few of them got stuck in trees in the area, but most of them disappeared."

"Sounds like fun," said Bolivia.

"It was. And it was exciting because the

Parents Association was going to give a prize to the student whose card was returned with a postmark from the farthest distance away."

"How far away did the balloons fly?" asked Bolivia.

"Most of the cards came back within a few days from other towns in New Jersey. There was a map in the hallway and whenever a student brought in their postcard, a star was placed on the map. Someone got their card mailed back to them from Delaware and someone else had a postmark from Philadelphia. Rory's card came back from Florida."

"Wow!" gasped Bolivia. "That's pretty far for a balloon to travel."

"You're right," said Derek. "And no one knew except me that Rory never attached his card to his balloon. Instead, he gave it to some neighbors of ours who were leaving for Miami that same day and asked them to mail it to him when they got there."

"So, you're saying he cheated," said Bolivia.

"Yes," said Derek. "And I cheated too

because I knew he did it and I didn't tell anyone. At least, I haven't told anyone until now. Rory won the prize, which was a pair of tickets to a hockey game in New York City, and he took me with him. And no one, not even his parents, guessed what he did."

"So you are an accessory to the crime," said Bolivia.

Derek nodded his head.

"Why didn't you tell?" asked Bolivia. "You could at least have refused to go to the game."

"Well, I wanted to see it. And besides, what was the point by then? It was old news. Balloon Day was in October and the hockey game was just two weeks ago," said Derek. "Only in the end I really didn't enjoy the game. I left feeling sick to my stomach, although I ate only one hot dog."

"It must have been your conscience," said Bolivia, nodding her head.

"Well, I never knew that my conscience was located in my stomach," said Derek. "But anyhow, if Rory could lie to the whole school

71

and the Parents Association, why wouldn't he lie to us?"

"You've got a point," said Bolivia. "I just don't believe that he would steal Hamlet. You're his best friend, after all."

Bolivia thought for a moment. "We'll have to set a trap for him and see if we can catch him. Then we'll know for sure."

"How can we do that?" asked Derek.

"What little things do you own that Rory likes? Things he might steal from you if he had a chance."

Derek thought hard. There was hardly anything he owned that Rory didn't have a duplicate of. "I don't know," he said.

"How about money? Do you have any money?" asked Bolivia.

"I have almost twenty dollars in the bank in my room," offered Derek. "I don't know if you noticed it on my bookshelf. It looks like a small safe. It even has a combination lock."

"Perfect," said Bolivia. "This afternoon we'll go to your house. Open the safe and leave the door ajar. If the money disappears, then we'll have our proof that Rory took everything."

"Good," said Derek. He felt relieved. He didn't want to discover that his best friend was a crook. But at least he wasn't alone anymore. He had confidence in Bolivia. If anyone could stop Rory from lying and stealing, it was Bolivia.

6
The Baited Trap

It wasn't hard to convince Rory that they had to spend the afternoon at Derek's house.

"We have to keep looking for Hamlet," Bolivia insisted before Rory could make a different suggestion. And so, with a morning of skating behind them and a lunch of Mrs. Dunn's homemade vegetable soup and grilled cheese sandwiches inside them, the three friends went to Derek's house.

"I'll keep Rory downstairs," Bolivia whispered to Derek when Rory wasn't listening. "You go open your safe."

Derek charged upstairs to his bedroom

and counted out the secret numbers to open the combination lock. Three to the right, seven to the left, and ten to the right. Only his father, who had given him the bank, knew the combination. Now the door was hanging open to trap Rory. It made Derek feel awful. He didn't want to tempt Rory and he didn't want to lose his money either.

Derek also felt terrible because Hamlet was still not in sight. He had wanted to believe Bolivia's idea that the hamster would return on his own to the cage. But when he peeked inside, the cage was empty.

Rory and Bolivia came up the stairs.

"Any sign of Hamlet?" asked Bolivia.

"None."

"Well, we won't give up. He's too small to open your front door. He's got to be in the house somewhere."

"But he's small enough to squeeze out of a small hole," suggested Rory. "He may have found a way outside."

Derek looked at Rory and wondered if the hole had been the opening of Rory's pants pocket. Was the hamster safely hidden away in Rory's bedroom two houses away?

"Let's split up," said Bolivia. "Rory, you look here in Derek's room. Derek, you look in your parents' bedroom and I'll look in the hallway. Be sure to check everywhere," she said as she pulled Derek by the sleeve out of his bedroom.

"We have to give Rory a chance to take the money," she whispered in Derek's ear when they were in the hallway outside of Derek's room.

Derek went into his parents' bedroom. He lay flat on the floor and tried to slide under their bed. There was no sign of Hamlet there. He got up and opened the closet door. He felt in all four corners of the closet floor but Hamlet was not hiding in any of them. He sat down on the floor and tried to imagine that he was a hamster. If he was, where would he go?

Downstairs, the door slammed shut. "Derek? Are you upstairs?" he heard his mother calling.

Derek looked at his watch. It was only three o'clock.

"Hi, Mom," Derek called back. He went to the top of the stairs. "How come you came home so early?" He went down the stairs to see his parents.

"Three different patients canceled their appointments for this afternoon. So here we are," Mrs. Curry explained to her son. "I guess no one wanted to see their dentist today."

"Rory and Bolivia are here with me," Derek told her. "We're looking for Hamlet. He's lost."

"He can't get far," said Dr. Curry. "I'm sure he'll turn up."

"Your father thought he'd take you kids out someplace as a treat," said Derek's mother. "But I think we better all see about locating that hamster first. Then if there's still time, you can go out later."

Derek shrugged his shoulders. He wasn't in the mood for treats. What kind of a friend was Rory anyhow, he wondered. He was probably up in his room stealing money out of his safe at this very moment.

"What's this on the floor?" asked Mrs.

Curry. She bent down and picked up a small piece of lettuce from the rug.

"We scattered some pieces of lettuce around to feed Hamlet," explained Bolivia, who had joined Derek downstairs. "We didn't want him to be hungry while he was lost."

"You have to eat at the table and Hamlet has to eat in his cage," said Mrs. Curry. "That's the rule around here." She noticed a second piece of lettuce and went to pick it up. "Otherwise, this house will become a pigsty."

"Or a lettuce field," giggled Bolivia.

"I still can't find your old hamster," called Rory, coming down the stairs to join the others.

"That hamster must be around the house somewhere," said Derek's father. "We'll all keep on searching until he is found."

"It's boring," Rory complained.

"You wouldn't like it if you were a hamster lost in this big house," pointed out Mrs. Curry.

Rory looked like he wanted to argue the point, but he didn't.

"I'm going to change my shoes," said

Derek's mother, "and then I'll help you look."

Derek, Rory, and Bolivia all sat down in the living room and waited. It was unlikely that Hamlet was downstairs. Derek knew he should continue looking upstairs but he felt as if he had searched every corner already.

Before Derek could go up to his room to look in his safe, he was startled by a piercing scream coming from his parents' room.

"What is it?" everyone called, running up the stairs to the bedroom. Dr. Curry was behind them, but he pushed ahead of the children and ran to his wife. "Are you all right?" he demanded.

Mrs. Curry was sitting on the bed. Her face was red and she was laughing.

"Look at this!" she called out. "I took off my work shoes and stuck my feet inside my slippers and there was company inside."

She held up Hamlet!

"I knew he would turn up," laughed Derek's father, sitting down on the bed and putting out his hand to take the animal.

"It's a good thing you didn't hurt him

when you stepped into your slipper," said Bolivia.

"I don't know what I thought it was, but it sure felt weird," said Mrs. Curry. "Did I scare you when I screamed? I scared myself," she admitted.

Derek took the hamster from his father. "It doesn't look as if you scared Hamlet," he said. "I'll put him where he belongs."

"Great," said his father. "And now there's still plenty of time for us to go to the Science Museum. They're having a new exhibit I think you'll enjoy. Then we can stop somewhere for a bite of supper, too, to celebrate the return of Hamlet."

Derek put the hamster carefully inside its cage and made certain that the door was securely shut.

"Okay, everyone," he heard his father calling. "Let's not waste any more time. Everyone inside the car."

Derek glanced up at his bookshelf. The safe door was still half open. He was just about to look inside his safe when Rory entered the room. There was no chance for

Derek to check the contents of his safe now.

Mrs. Curry stuck her head into the room, too. "Come on, guys," she said. "Better get a move on."

Derek and Rory went downstairs and put on their jackets. Bolivia was standing by the door waiting for them. She raised her eyebrows in an inquiring manner but Derek could only shrug his shoulders. He didn't know yet if Rory had fallen into the trap they had set for him. But come to think of it, if Hamlet was safe and Rory hadn't stolen him after all, maybe his friend wasn't the thief he had thought he was.

"Just a minute," said Dr. Curry, and he went back upstairs for something he had forgotten.

The kids piled into the car to wait for him. Derek sat next to Rory. Suddenly he was feeling much better about things. Hamlet had been found. He grinned at his friend. Best friends don't steal from each other. Bolivia's knife was most likely somewhere in the Goldings' house. He was ashamed of himself for being so suspicious of Rory. He would have to make it up to him somehow.

Dr. Curry drove to the Science Museum. The new exhibit that he wanted them to see was all about teeth and fangs. No wonder his dentist father had been so eager to come here. They walked about the museum learning about how teeth helped animals chew and eat. There was a short film showing a beaver colony at work.

"You'd think they'd get splinters in their tongues," Bolivia commented, making a face.

Afterward, they all had hamburgers and salad at a local diner before returning home. It had been a good afternoon.

Back in his room, Derek peeked into his bank before locking it. Earlier in the afternoon there had been two five-dollar bills and nine singles. Now, although there was still some loose change inside the safe, the bills were gone. *Rory had stolen the money after all.*

Derek sat on his bed, stunned. His pleasure was forgotten. His best friend had just stolen all of his money. His *former* best friend! He didn't want to have anything to do with Rory anymore.

7
A Red-Hot Rage

After discovering that his money had been stolen, Derek sat on his bed, getting angrier by the minute. At least I have Hamlet back, he thought. Rory didn't get him after all.

Derek thought back to the events of that afternoon. Was it possible that Rory had stolen the hamster and then returned it when they came to the house for their afternoon search?

He wasn't going to wait until tomorrow to get his questions answered, Derek decided. Besides, he wanted his money back right now.

"I'm going over to Rory's house," he shouted to his parents as he put on his jacket.

"Now? You just spent the whole day with him," protested his mother. "And you'll see him again in the morning."

"This is important," Derek called as the door banged behind him.

As he passed the Goldings' house on his way to Rory's, he decided to tell Bolivia what had happened. After all, she had been the one with the idea of trapping Rory. She should know that the bait had indeed caught him.

Mr. Golding opened the door. "For goodness' sake," said the old man. "You kids can't seem to bear being separated."

"This is important," Derek explained. "I have to talk with Bolivia."

Bolivia must have heard his voice because she appeared in the doorway. "What's up?" she asked.

"I have to speak to you in private," he explained.

"Young man, if you have come to propose

to my niece, you must ask my permission first."

"Stop teasing him," said Mrs. Golding, who had joined the others at the door. "Come in, Derek. Why don't you and Bolivia go in the kitchen? We'll be in the living room," she added as she pulled her husband by the arm.

When they were alone in the kitchen, Derek spoke. "The money's gone," he said. "I checked my bank and the money is gone. Rory took it."

"Have you talked to him yet?"

"No," said Derek. "I'm on my way over now. And I'm not leaving his house until I get my money back."

"I'll go with you," offered Bolivia. "I'm a witness that you left the bank open this afternoon."

"All right," agreed Derek. He was glad not to have to face Rory alone. It wasn't very nice to have to accuse your former best friend of being a criminal. But it wasn't very nice of him to have stolen the money either.

"I'll be back in a couple of minutes," Bolivia

called to the Goldings. "I'm just going over to Rory's house." She grabbed her jacket and she and Derek ran outside before Mr. Golding had time to make another joke.

Rory opened the door when they rang the bell. "Hi!" he said. He seemed surprised to see his two friends standing outside the door of his home at nine o'clock in the evening.

"I have to talk to you in private," said Derek as he came inside.

"Then why did you bring Bolivia?" asked a puzzled Rory.

"I'm a witness," Bolivia explained.

The three went upstairs to Rory's room. Rory's mother saw them walking up the stairs and called out to them. "Derek, did you or Bolivia see my wristwatch lying around when you were here at lunchtime? I remember placing it on the kitchen counter because I was going to take it to the jeweler this afternoon to get a new battery for it. And now it's disappeared."

"I didn't see it," Bolivia called to Mrs. Dunn.

"This is getting ridiculous," Derek said as they closed the door to Rory's room. "Nothing is safe anymore. Everything is disappearing."

"What are you talking about?" asked Rory.

"I'm talking about your mother's watch and Bolivia's Swiss army knife and my hamster and now my nineteen dollars. You're going to end up in jail if you keep this up. But first I want my money back."

"What money? I don't know what you're talking about," said Rory.

"Rory, it's better to admit it now that you have been caught," said Bolivia softly. "Just give Derek his money and give me my knife, and if you promise never to steal anything from us again, we'll forgive you."

"I didn't steal anything from you," said Rory, his face turning red.

"I had nineteen dollars in my safe this afternoon," said Derek. "I left the door open and now the money is gone. You took it. And I want it back. Now."

"If you left the door open, it's no wonder

your money is gone. But I wasn't the one who took it. And I don't know why you think I did."

"Because I've heard you lying to people all fall. Because no one can trust you anymore. Because if you lie to other people, why wouldn't you lie to me, too?"

Derek grabbed Rory and stuck his hand into the pockets of his friend's jeans. "Come on, where is the money?"

"Hey, stop it!" Rory shouted, pushing Derek away. "You can't do this."

"Yes, I can," said Derek. He turned from Rory and pulled open the top drawer of his chest. "Where did you hide my money?" he demanded. He grabbed a handful of Rory's underwear and threw it on the floor. "I know my money is somewhere in this room."

Rory tried to pull Derek away from the drawers. When he was unable to move him, he kicked Derek behind his left knee.

"That's dirty fighting!" shouted Bolivia.

Derek reached over and turned on Rory's radio. Loud. He didn't want Rory's parents to

hear what was going on. He just wanted to get his money and leave.

He opened the door to Rory's closet. "Is it in here?" he asked.

"I didn't steal your money!" Rory shouted above the music. "I don't need your old money and besides, why would I take it from you?"

"For the same reason that you took Bolivia's knife. And the same reason that you cheated at Balloon Day at school. When you want something, you don't worry about whether it's honest or dishonest."

"Come off it!" yelled Rory. He looked close to tears. "Balloon Day has nothing to do with any of this. Anybody at school would have done what I did if they had thought of it. And what does that have to do with Bolivia losing her knife?"

Derek turned from the closet. The floor of Rory's room was covered with underwear and T-shirts, shoes and boxed games.

"You don't seem to understand," said Derek. "You are a criminal! People go to jail for the things you do."

Rory sat down on his bed. He shouted above the blaring music, "I did not steal Bolivia's knife! I swear it. It was a neat knife and I'm sorry it got lost. I liked it. Maybe someday I'll buy one for myself. But I did not take hers. You've got to believe me."

"If you didn't take it, who did?" asked Derek. "And how are you planning to get one for yourself? With my money?"

"If you're stupid enough to leave your bank open and your money gets stolen, it's your fault. I don't see why you are blaming me. Bolivia was in your house this afternoon. Maybe she stole the money. Did you ever think of that?" asked Rory.

"Me?" shouted Bolivia. "Why would I steal Derek's money?"

"So you could buy yourself another knife?" said Rory.

Derek looked from Bolivia to Rory. He hadn't thought of it. Maybe Bolivia had stolen his money. After all, she knew the safe was open. She could have taken it.

"Did you ever think that maybe Derek took your knife?" Rory asked Bolivia. "He liked it a lot when you showed it to us. Why couldn't he have taken it and then blamed me?"

Derek looked at Rory with shock. How could Rory say a thing like that?

"What's going on up here?" called Mrs. Dunn, coming into Rory's room. "The music on your radio is much too loud! It's going to wake Edna. . . ." She paused as she saw the chaos in her son's room. "What in the world are you doing?" she asked Rory.

"Nothing," he said, turning off the radio.

"We're just looking for something," explained Derek.

"You're not going to bed until you put this room back in order," said Mrs. Dunn to her son. "And you'd better hurry because it's getting late," she said as she left the room.

Rory turned to Derek and Derek turned to Bolivia. No one wanted to clean up the room.

"I'll give you until tomorrow morning to return my money," said Derek, looking at the two of them. "One of you has it. And whoever it is better return it. Otherwise, I'll tell my parents."

Bolivia grabbed a handful of Rory's underwear and stuffed it back into one of the drawers. "I can't believe that you think I took it," she said. "I'm the one who told you how to trap Rory." She kicked a pair of Rory's shoes into the closet.

"What kind of friend are you?" Rory asked Bolivia. "Looking for ways to *trap* me. I can't believe you guys. This is unreal."

In a few minutes Rory's room seemed to be back in order. There was nothing on the floor that didn't belong there. But nothing in his drawers or in his closet was in the right place. As Derek left Rory's house, he still didn't know who had stolen his money. Rory said it was Bolivia. Bolivia said it was Rory. And Derek thought it could just as easily be either one. Neither he nor Bolivia spoke to each other.

Derek went home to bed but it was a long time before he fell asleep. It was probably the second-worst night of his life. The worst had been when he was six years old and knew that the next morning he was going to the hospital to have his tonsils removed. On second thought, the hospital hadn't been that terrible. *This* was the worst night of Derek's life.

8
Bolivia Packs Her Bags

Derek slept late the following morning. And when he woke he felt a heavy, unpleasant feeling inside. It took a moment to remember what was bothering him—the fight last night with both Rory and Bolivia.

The door to his bank was open, reminding him of the missing money. He wondered who had stolen it, Rory or Bolivia. Then he remembered Rory's accusation that he had taken Bolivia's knife. Even brushing his teeth with the new chocolate toothpaste did not improve the bad taste in Derek's mouth or his sour mood.

Because he had overslept, his parents had

already left for work. There was a note on the kitchen table:

Derek,

Here is money to pick up half a dozen bagels. Better get them first thing, so you don't forget! Mrs. Dunn is expecting you to have lunch with Rory. See you around 5:30.

Love,
Mom

Derek read the note twice. He didn't feel like eating breakfast, and he certainly wouldn't go and have lunch at Rory's house.

Leaving the pot of cooked cereal on the stove untouched, Derek put on his jacket and went out to buy the bagels for his mother. As he left the house, he felt a few soft flakes of snow beginning to fall.

Mrs. Golding opened her window and called to Derek as he walked past the house. "What happened with you kids last night?" she demanded.

Derek reluctantly walked over toward the window. "Just a minute. I'm going to catch pneumonia if I don't put my coat on," Mrs. Golding called to him. A moment later, her door opened and the older woman came outside.

"Bolivia insists she wants to go home this morning. I can't understand it. She was here all summer and she never got homesick for one minute. She was fine yesterday evening, until she went over to Rory's house with you. What happened? You had a fight, didn't you?"

"Sort of," admitted Derek. He was stunned by Mrs. Golding's announcement. It had never occurred to him that Bolivia would go home early.

"Well, why don't you go in and apologize to her? I've been on the phone to the airline trying to change her flight. But I hate to have her leave like this—especially when you've been such good friends up until now."

"Why don't you talk to Rory?" asked Derek. "It's all his fault. At least I think it is." At that moment Derek wasn't certain about anything. The snow was coming down heavily now and he wiped some off his face.

"I've got to go to the store for my mother," he said and turned away from Mrs. Golding. He thought about Bolivia packing her things to go home.

The bagel shop was three blocks away. By the time he got there snow was already accumulating in a thick layer on top of cars and on the street. Inside the store, the yeasty aroma of the freshly baked dough smelled good. It reminded Derek that he hadn't eaten any breakfast. He wished he had enough money for an extra bagel to eat on the way home. He decided that his mother wouldn't object if he ate just half of one.

"How many?" asked the man behind the counter.

"Six," Derek responded.

"Six plain?"

Derek nodded and then watched as the man pulled out an enormous paper bag from under the counter and began filling it. When he saw pumpernickel bagels and sesame bagels and raisin bagels going into the bag, he realized that the man was filling a different

98

order. Derek's stomach gave a growl of protest. It was used to having a regular meal first thing in the morning.

"Can you manage this?" asked the man as he pushed the huge bag over the top of the counter toward Derek. And then he gave Derek a second, equally large bag.

Derek looked puzzled. "I only asked for six," he said, eyeing the gigantic assortment of bagels the man was offering him.

"I just got a call from my boss. He said to turn off the ovens and lock up. They are predicting a real humdinger of a storm and I have a long ride home."

"I don't have enough money," said Derek.

"Listen, sonny. If you don't take these they'll just go stale sitting in the store. They're a present. Merry Christmas."

Derek was stunned by the unexpected gift. "Gosh. Thanks," he said.

"You'd better hurry home," the man advised him.

"I live only a few blocks away," Derek explained. He took the bags and started out

the door. In the short time that he had been inside the shop, the wind had begun to blow really hard. It pushed against him as he started walking. Derek had planned to eat a bagel as he walked, but the wind was blowing so hard that he couldn't stand still and he needed both hands to hold on to the bags. He had to concentrate on where he was walking. It was hard to see with the wind blowing snow into his eyes.

Going home took Derek at least twice the amount of time that walking to the bakery did. Cars moved very slowly on the streets and there were only a couple of other people walking outside.

When he finally reached his street, Rory was shoveling a path through the snow in front of his house. Rory looked up as Derek passed, but for the first time ever, neither boy greeted the other.

Derek shifted the heavy bags in his arms and kept on walking till he reached his own house. It wasn't easy getting his key out of his pocket while holding the two heavy bags, but he kept his back turned toward Rory. He wasn't going to ask him for help.

Derek finally found the key and opened the door. He went inside with the bags, making wet tracks as he walked to the kitchen. Then, after he removed his boots and jacket, Derek pulled a bagel out of one of the bags.

As he chewed, he went to the window and looked out. He could see Rory still shoveling the snow in front of his house. The snow was falling so heavily now that no sooner was an area cleared than it was covered with fresh snow. Once, a couple of years ago when they were younger, he and Rory had tried making an igloo when there had been a big snow-storm. It would be fun to be out in such a heavy snow, if he had someone to play with.

Derek finished his bagel and went to pour himself a glass of orange juice. He took a second bagel, and then dumped out the contents of the two bags and counted them. There were seventy bagels left. The man had given him six dozen bagels! A week ago this would have been fabulous: all these bagels to eat with his friends and all that snow outside to play in.

He thought about Bolivia and wondered if she would come to Woodside next summer. Probably not, he decided. She had never visited Woodside until last summer and it was because of her good friendship with Rory and himself that she had wanted to come back now. If she left while they were in the middle of a fight, she would never come back.

Then Derek remembered what Rory had said about Bolivia stealing his money. It really was possible that she was the thief. She was the one who knew that the door to the safe was open. And she knew that he would blame Rory if the money was gone.

Derek walked to the living room and turned on the television set. He turned the dial looking for something that would be fun to watch, and finally settled for a quiz show. He watched as the contestants jumped up and down screaming and cheering like maniacs whenever they guessed a correct answer.

Just as a tall man from Irving, Texas, was trying to name the twelfth President of the United States, the front door opened and Derek's parents walked in, covered with snow.

"How come you're home already?" Derek asked with surprise.

"It's a real blizzard out there," said his mother, breathing heavily as she tried to catch her breath. "We canceled all our patients and tried to drive home, but the visibility is so poor we had to abandon the car and walk most of the way."

"They're predicting that the snow will continue until late tonight," Derek's father said. "We may get as much as twenty inches!"

"This is an absolute waste of snow," Derek complained. "If we had school they would close it, and we would get to spend a day at home. But we're already home because it is a vacation. It's not fair."

"My goodness!" shrieked Mrs. Curry from the kitchen. "What is all this?"

She was looking at all the bagels on the

kitchen table. "How many did you buy?"

"Six, but the man gave me the rest. He said he was closing the store because of the storm and that if I didn't take them they would just go stale."

"They'll go stale here, too," said Derek's father. "There's no way three people can eat all those. And I don't think we could fit them all in the freezer, either."

"I have a great idea," said Mrs. Curry. "I'll invite the Dunns and the Goldings and some of our other neighbors over for a blizzard party. I'll serve bagels and whatever else I can scare up."

Derek made a face. On any other day the idea of a party would have been great. But the thought of having the Dunns, together with Rory, and the Goldings without Bolivia, did not appeal to him at all.

"Don't be a party pooper," Mrs. Curry said, seeing the expression on her son's face. And she went off to the telephone to call their friends.

"Is something bothering you?" Derek's father asked him.

Derek shook his head. He didn't want to talk about it. Then seeing that his father was still watching him and waiting for him to respond, he thought of something to say.

"Dad, do you know who was the twelfth President of the United States?"

9
The Blizzard
Party

By two o'clock that afternoon there were
six inches of snow outside and sixty-
seven bagels inside on the kitchen table in
Derek's house. Derek had thought he would
eat one of each kind but by the time he had a
poppyseed bagel and a pumpernickel bagel
on top of a plain bagel, he was full. He didn't
think he'd want to eat another for a week. His
parents had each eaten one as part of their
lunch.

Derek lay on the living-room floor watching one stupid television program after another. Mrs. Curry came into the room and
switched off the set. "Enough TV," she said.

"Where's Rory? How come you fellows aren't playing out in the snow? And where's Bolivia?"

"She flew home," said Derek, responding only to the last of his mother's questions.

"Flew home? That's impossible. The airport is shut down. The snow drifts are so high that the runways are covered with snow as soon as they are plowed clear."

"Really?" said Derek, sitting up. "I didn't know that."

"I just heard it on the radio," his mother told him.

For a moment Derek felt a twinge of pleasure. So Bolivia hadn't gone home after all. That was great! But then he remembered again that she might very well have stolen his money. And if she hadn't gone home, then it meant that she would be coming with the Goldings to have supper at his house in the evening.

"Please shovel our walk," Mrs. Curry told Derek. "Your father shoveled an hour ago, but with all this snow and wind you'd never know it."

Derek put on his boots and his warm jacket. He looked around for a different woolen cap. What had he worn before he received the striped one from Bolivia? He couldn't remember and he couldn't find it. So he was forced to wear Bolivia's gift on his head.

Outside, the cold air revived Derek and temporarily lifted his spirits. He shoveled great clumps of snow off the path. On either side of the walk the piles of snow were easily a foot high. The cars parked along the curb-side were totally covered and looked like small mountains. The hedges and shrubs in the yards up and down the street were also covered. Best of all, the snow was falling as heavily as ever and didn't give any sign that it would ever stop.

When he finished shoveling the walk, Derek decided that he would build a snow-man in front of his house. He would make it twice as big as the snow person that he and Rory and Bolivia had built earlier in the week. He set to work and had already made the bottom portion of his figure when he turned and noticed that Bolivia was standing outside the Goldings' house. She too was busy building a snow figure—a companion to the first that still stood at the entrance to the Goldings'.

Derek pretended that he didn't see her. He continued working on his snowman. And when he looked up again he could see Rory working, busy building a snowman outside his house. Except for the occasional scraping sound of a shovel, it was quiet as the three worked on their projects. Derek was determined that his snowman would be larger than Rory's or Bolivia's.

By five o'clock there were ten inches of snow on the ground and it was coming down as heavily as ever. "They have revised the forecast," Derek's father announced. "We will probably get twenty-four inches before it is over."

Because of the strong winds there were drifts much higher than twenty-four inches already. Mrs. Curry watched the early news as she prepared a pot of split pea soup for her guests. There was footage of abandoned cars on all the major highways. The scenes of Newark Airport showed enormous drifts of snow. Underneath some of those drifts were airplanes.

Local restaurants and stores had taken in stranded passengers and pedestrians. There was a shot of a pizza parlor filled with customers who had come in out of the snow. "We ran out of pepperoni!" shouted the store's owner. "But we have plenty of dough." In one hand he held a ball of pizza dough and in the other a fistful of bills. He was enjoying the snow or at least the results of it.

Rory came over with his parents. Edna was jumping up and down with excitement. "The snow is bigger than me!" she shouted delightedly.

Mrs. Dunn brought two packages of frankfurters that had been in her freezer. Derek's mother cut them up into the pea soup. Rory looked about self-consciously. Obviously, he didn't want to be at this party. Derek made a point of helping his mother set the table and carry up some folding chairs from the basement. Anything, so he wouldn't have to stay in the same room with Rory.

The Kimbles from down the street came bringing a huge jar of homemade applesauce. They had tickets to fly to Florida for seven o'clock that evening. Now they were not going on their vacation and they had no food in the house, either. "I'll give you our leftovers to see you through the storm," Mrs. Curry promised them. "We have plenty of bagels!"

The Goldings arrived last, bringing Bolivia and a huge plateful of oatmeal raisin cookies. Bolivia stared straight ahead. She didn't look at either Derek or Rory but went right over to Edna. It was good there were so many guests in the house, Derek thought. That way, no one would notice that he wasn't paying any attention to Rory and Bolivia, and that they were ignoring him, too.

When they sat down to eat, the three managed to sit as far away from each other as possible. Derek carefully looked only at the food and not at them. But from time to time he would glance quickly to see if either Rory or Bolivia was looking at him. They weren't.

"I wish it would snow every day forever," said Edna as they were all eating. She was holding a bagel in one hand and pea soup dribbled down her chin. Nobody over the age of eleven agreed with Edna.

Suddenly, Dr. Curry called to his son across the table. "Oh, Derek," he said. "With all this snow I completely forgot to get to the bank this morning. I didn't have very much cash on me when we were going to the museum yesterday afternoon, so I borrowed the money you had in your little safe bank."

Derek was so stunned by his father's unexpected comment that he choked on a mouthful of soup. Mr. Golding leaned over and slapped him hard on the back. "Take it easy," he said. "Hold your arms up over your head."

Derek's face turned a bright red. The adults at the table thought it was from coughing but Rory and Bolivia knew the real cause.

It had never occurred to Derek or any of them that one of Derek's parents was guilty of taking the money. How could they have had so little faith in one another?

Derek looked sheepishly toward his friends

who were sitting across the table. Rory grinned and Bolivia winked at him. It was all Derek could do to contain himself. He wanted to jump up and down and shout "Wowee! Wowee!" the way the man did on the quiz show. What was winning a free set of luggage or a trip to Hawaii compared to knowing that you had friends you could trust?

After a while Edna got down from the table and looked out the window at the snow. Derek's father left the table and built a fire in the living-room fireplace. Derek loved it when his father used the fireplace. It didn't really heat the house, but everything looked so cozy in the firelight. It smelled good, too.

Rory's mother and Mrs. Kimble helped clear the table while Derek's mother put on a pot of coffee. The others left the table and sat in the living room together. There were not enough chairs or space on the sofa for everyone, so Derek, Rory, and Bolivia went upstairs.

"I'm sorry I accused you of taking my money," Derek said to Rory when they were

in the bedroom. It wasn't easy to say, but he knew he had to say it.

"I told you I didn't take it," Rory responded. "Why didn't you believe me?"

Bolivia turned and faced Rory. "Derek told me what you did with that postcard that was supposed to be attached to the balloon."

Rory blushed. "You weren't supposed to tell anyone," he accused Derek.

"I'm not just anyone!" said Bolivia. "Besides, you see how doing something like that made it possible for Derek to believe you stole his money?"

"It's like the story of the boy who cried wolf," said Derek, remembering the Aesop's fable they had learned at school years ago.

Rory nodded thoughtfully. "It was stupid," he admitted. "I didn't really enjoy that hockey game at all. At the time it seemed like such a good idea to get those free tickets, but in the end I felt awful that I cheated."

"Did you throw up when you came home? I did," said Derek.

"Me, too," admitted Rory.

"Promise that you'll make a New Year's resolution: no more lying or cheating," said Bolivia, looking at the boys. "I can't be friends with anyone I can't trust—or who doesn't trust me," she added.

Derek remembered how, for at least a little while, he had thought that she had taken his money.

"I agree," said Rory, holding out his hand. They shook on it three ways.

"I guess you're going to have to stick around another couple of days," Derek said to Bolivia. "The airport is totally buried under snowdrifts."

"Yep," Bolivia agreed. She didn't seem at all unhappy about it.

"We won't be able to go ice skating," Rory pointed out. "The rink is buried under snow, but we can go sledding."

"When the snow stops we can shovel people's walks and help them dig out their cars," suggested Bolivia. "We'll make a fortune."

Derek lay back on the bedroom rug and listened to Bolivia and Rory talking. They were counting up the number of people who would want their services. A few families had their own kids to do the work for them, but there were many who would be in need of help.

Now that Hamlet was safe in his cage and he knew where his money was, there was still one unsolved mystery, thought Derek. He wondered where Bolivia's Swiss army knife was. Somehow, just as he had once been certain that Rory had stolen it, he was now certain that he hadn't. That meant that the knife had gotten really lost.

Derek had a plan. When Bolivia went down to the kitchen to get them some cookies, he leaned over and whispered to Rory.

"Let's chip in together and buy Bolivia a new knife like the one she lost. We'll make plenty of money shoveling snow."

"I can't believe it," Rory sputtered in amazement. "I was just going to tell you the same thing."

"What were you going to tell him?" asked Bolivia as she handed each of the boys one of the oatmeal raisin cookies.

Rory took a huge bite of cookie to stall for time. Derek waited to see what his friend would say. "I was going to say that if it hadn't snowed, this would have been a rotten Christmas vacation," said Rory.

10
Good-bye, Again

After two days the weather turned hot. Outside it was at least forty degrees and the radio announcer forecast that the temperature would rise to the mid-fifties before the day was over.

"It's a regular heat wave outside," joked Derek's father as he got ready to go to his office.

"Poor Mrs. Elgin," said his wife. She turned to Derek. "Mrs. Elgin was scheduled to have an abscessed tooth removed the day of the snowstorm. She's been taking aspirin and waiting for us to reopen the office."

Derek knew it must have hurt waiting the

extra days with an aching tooth. Still, if the snow hadn't come, Bolivia would have gone. Now with the improved weather Mrs. Elgin would get relief from her pain. And Bolivia would return home. It was funny how good news for one person could mean bad news for someone else.

Derek said good-bye to his parents and decided to go over to Rory's. Then the two of them could say good-bye to Bolivia. Derek didn't know if he wanted to ride to the airport to see her off or not. It had been fun welcoming Bolivia. Saying good-bye was not something he looked forward to doing. He felt inside his pocket for the Swiss army knife that his father had managed to pick up for him the day before. He knew Bolivia would be pleased when he presented her with this unexpected wrapped gift.

Rory opened the door the moment Derek pushed the bell.

"Bolivia is here," he said.

Derek followed Rory inside. Bolivia was sitting at the kitchen table, watching Edna finish her breakfast.

"I'll come back again," Bolivia was promising the little girl.

"When?" asked Edna.

"Maybe in the summer," Bolivia told her.

"Will it be summer next week?" asked Edna.

"Not for many weeks," said Bolivia. "But it will come when all the snow melts and the weather gets hot again."

Mrs. Dunn came into the kitchen. She greeted her son's friends. "We're sorry to have you leave Woodside," she said to Bolivia. "But I'm sure you'll be back again before we know it."

"Actually, I think it's time for Rory and Derek to come visit me," said Bolivia.

Derek and Rory exchanged glances. Visiting Bolivia—that would be something really special.

"And me too! Me too!" Edna shouted. She didn't want to be left out.

Derek looked at Rory, watching for a signal. He caught his friend's eye and Rory nodded back. He put his hand inside his pocket and pulled out the small package.

"This is for you," he said. "It's from Rory and me."

"Another Christmas present?" asked Bolivia in surprise. "Gee, thanks," she said as she tore the paper off the small box and opened it. Inside was a Swiss army knife exactly like the one she had lost.

"Oh," shouted Bolivia with surprise. "I forgot to show you." She put her hand in her pocket and pulled out a twin to the knife that the boys had given her.

"You found it?" asked Derek in amazement. "Where was it? I can't believe that you really found it after all our hunting."

"I didn't find it," said Bolivia. "My aunt and uncle gave me this last night to replace the one that got lost. Now I guess I have two," she laughed.

Rory and Derek looked at the two knives on the table. It didn't seem fair that they had spent their hard-earned money from shoveling snow to buy Bolivia a new knife if her relatives had already replaced the missing one.

"I have a knife, too," said Edna.

Bolivia picked up the butter knife that was resting on the table. "Yes, you do," she agreed.

"Not that one," said Edna, shaking her head. "I have a red one just like you."

She climbed down from her chair and ran out of the room. A minute later she returned holding a piece of Christmas wrapping paper. She opened the paper and inside was a Swiss army knife.

"You had it?" gasped Rory. "You had Bolivia's knife all this time!"

"I have lots of things," said Edna proudly.

"Do you have my can opener?" asked Rory's mother. "It's been missing for days."

"What else do you have?" asked Bolivia curiously. "Will you show me?"

Edna shook her head and smiled. "It's the game," she reminded Bolivia. "It's the new game that you taught me."

Bolivia followed Edna to her bedroom. Derek and Rory and Mrs. Dunn followed, too. It seemed as if a lot of mysteries were suddenly going to be cleared up.

Sure enough, in the corner of Edna's closet,

underneath her old security blanket that she hardly ever used anymore, there was a pile of treasures. Most were crudely wrapped in paper. There was a bar of soap, two forks, one of Mrs. Dunn's black satin evening shoes, a Christmas tree ornament, a handful of coins, and Mrs. Dunn's missing wristwatch.

"I did a good job of hiding them," said Edna, beaming. "You never found them."

"I didn't even know this was missing," said Mrs. Dunn, picking up her shoe. "Why did you take them?"

"It's the game," said Edna.

"It's all my fault," said Bolivia. "Remember when we played Boxing Day? Edna never stopped playing."

"So she was the one who took the knife," said Derek, feeling awful all over again that he had once been so sure that Rory had done it.

"That means now you have three knives," commented Rory.

"I don't need three," said Bolivia. She handed one to Derek and one to Rory. "Now we each have one," she said.

The boys stroked the shiny red plastic of their knives. It was great that now they each had one. And what wonderful adventures they could have now that they were prepared for everything.

"I want one!" shrieked Edna.

"Little girls don't play with knives," soothed her mother, picking her up.

"It's lucky she didn't get hurt," said Derek.

"She wouldn't have been able to open it," said Bolivia. "You need strong fingers to pull out the blades."

"I want a red knife, too," sobbed Edna.

"We'll get you something else that is red and that is better for a girl your age," said Mrs. Dunn. "But you must promise me that you won't hide any more of our things. You can't play this game anymore, do you understand?"

Edna nodded.

"Edna, did you take my little flashlight?" Rory asked his sister suddenly. "I was looking all over for it the other day but I couldn't find it."

Edna shook her head. And Derek remembered that this time he was the thief. He would return the flashlight to Rory later and explain how he happened to have it.

"Let's play a better game," said Bolivia. "Did you ever play sardines?"

"Sardines?" asked Derek, wrinkling his nose in disgust. Sardines were those smelly little fish that came in a can. His father liked to eat them for lunch sometimes on a Saturday. But Derek wouldn't eat one if his life depended on it. "What kind of a game can you make out of sardines?" he asked.

"It's like hide-and-seek, only more fun," said Bolivia. "In this game just one person hides and everyone else goes looking. Whoever finds the hidden person, hides with him. Then the next person who finds both of them hides there, too. They get all squished together hiding, just like sardines in a can. And eventually everyone is hiding except the last one who is still looking."

Leave it to Bolivia to come up with the perfect game, Derek thought as he covered his eyes and began silently counting to a hundred. Bolivia was hiding and they were all going to look for her.

By the time Derek located Bolivia's hiding place behind the sofa, he had to squeeze in with Rory. "Who's looking for us now?" he whispered.

"My aunt and uncle," giggled Bolivia. Sure enough, Derek could hear their voices at the front door.

"Bolivia! Rory! Derek!" called Mrs. Dunn. "The Goldings are ready to leave for the airport."

"Shhhh," whispered Bolivia. "Let's see if they can find us."

"The kids are playing a kind of hide-and-seek," said Mrs. Dunn. She brought the Goldings into the living room and asked them to sit down. It was hard not to laugh as they felt the vibrations when the adults sat down on the sofa.

"Bolivia!" Mrs. Dunn shouted again.

"She's here!" shouted Edna. "I found her! I found everybody."

The children all climbed out from behind the sofa.

"I'm sorry. It's time to go," said Mrs. Golding.

"I know," said Bolivia. "We were just playing one last game."

"We don't have time for games," said Mrs. Golding. "This isn't like last time when you were just pretending. Your plane is really about to go."

"Pretending?" asked Rory and Derek together.

"Sure," said Mrs. Golding. "You don't think I would let Bolivia leave before her visit was up, do you? And besides, her parents were out of town, so where would she go? But she said she wanted me to tell you she was going home early. So that's what I said."

Bolivia grinned wickedly. "I thought I'd shake you guys up a little," she said. "But what with the snowstorm and everything, it hardly mattered."

"What about telling the truth?" asked Rory.

"You're right," Bolivia agreed. "I shook hands on it, didn't I? Okay, no more fooling around. Cross my heart and hope to die."

"Time to go," said Mrs. Golding. "Are you fellows coming along for the ride to the airport?"

"Sure," both Derek and Rory answered together.

"Promise that you'll write to me," said Bolivia when they were at the airline terminal and she was about to board her plane.

"There's never anything to write about. Nothing ever happens here," Rory complained.

"At least, nothing happens when you're not around," said Derek.

"Something's got to happen sometimes," Bolivia insisted. "Write!"

She kissed her aunt and uncle good-bye and waved to the boys. They watched as she walked through the gate away from them toward the entrance to her plane. And after the plane took off, they took off too, back to Woodside.

The rest of the day, the last day of their

winter vacation, passed slowly. Even board games and television programs weren't any fun without Bolivia.

Then, late in the afternoon, Edna showed Rory and Derek that she had found one more gift-wrapped package that hadn't been discovered earlier in the day.

"What do you have now?" asked Rory.

Edna opened the box and pulled out the missing can opener.

"You had it?" laughed Mrs. Dunn. And the others laughed, too.

"Now we have something to write to Bolivia about after all," said Derek. And he rushed off to find a sheet of notepaper.

PALOS WEST LIBRARY
12700 South 104th Avenue
Palos Park, Ill. 60464

132